Matt Dickinson is a writer and film-maker.

His books for adults include *The Death Zone*, *Black Ice* and *High Risk*. His books for young adults include the *Mortal Chaos* series, *The Everest Files* trilogy and *Lie, Kill, Walk Away*. His most recent series, *Popcorn-Eating Squirrels*, is for younger children.

He is also the author of Diffusion's book *Snake*.

As a film-maker, Matt has worked extensively for National Geographic Television, the Discovery Channel and the BBC. He is one of very few people to have ever filmed on the summit of Mount Everest.

About Diffusion books

Diffusion publishes books for adults who are emerging readers. There are two series:

Books in the Diamond series are ideally suited to those who are relatively new to reading or who have not practised their reading skills for some time (approximately Entry Level 2 to 3 in adult literacy levels).

Books in the Star series are for those who are ready for the next step. These books will help to build confidence and inspire readers to tackle longer books (approximately Entry Level 3 to Level 1 in adult literacy levels).

Books available in the Diamond series are:

Space Ark by Rob Childs

Flare Up by Matt Dickinson

Snake by Matt Dickinson

Fans by Niall Griffiths

Breaking the Chain by Darren Richards

Lost at Sea by Joel Smith

Uprising by Alex Wheatle

Books available in the Star series are:

Forty-six Quid and a Bag of Dirty Washing by Andy Croft

Bare Freedom by Andy Croft

Nowhere to Run by Michael Crowley

Not Such a Bargain by Toby Forward

Barcelona Away by Tom Palmer

One Shot by Lena Semaan

For more information, visit:

www.diffusionbooks.org.uk

Flare Up

Matt Dickinson

First published in Great Britain in 2021

Diffusion
an imprint of SPCK
36 Causton Street
London
SW1P 4ST
www.diffusionbooks.org.uk

ISBN 978-1-908713-27-8

Typeset by Nord Compo
Printed and bound in Great Britain by Ashford Colour Press.
Subsequently digitally reprinted in Great Britain

Produced on paper from sustainable forests

Contents

1
A surprise visitor

Wind and hailstones were beating against the window of Jason's flat that morning. The weather in Aberdeen was hard in winter.

Jason groaned as he woke up. His head was fuzzy, and his left eye was swollen and sore.

The fuzzy head was down to a couple of pints of beer over the limit the night before. The swollen eye was down to a couple of right-handers a short time later.

He remembered a scuffle in the gutter. He had been in a late-night brawl.

It was not just the bruises that made Jason's cheeks glow. It was the shame as well. He could not even remember why he had got into a fight.

The doorbell rang. The noise felt like a drill screwing into Jason's brain.

He stumbled out of bed. He looked around the flat for some clean clothes, but could not find any. The washing machine had been broken for weeks.

That wasn't all. Things had changed since Jason's girlfriend had chucked him out and he was living on his own. He had got into some bad ways.

Borrowing money from mates. Then not paying it back.

Gambling online because he was bored.

The doorbell rang again.

'All right!' he shouted.

He opened the door and found a friendly face. It was Mac. His uncle.

Jason smiled. Mac was a legend. He had been in the Navy when he was younger, but now he was a diver. He worked on the oil rigs in the North Sea. It was dangerous work but big money.

Mac had always been good to Jason. He never forgot Jason's birthday. He helped Jason when he could.

'Hi,' Jason said. 'Come in and sit down. Don't mind the mess.'

Mac removed some dirty plates from the sofa so he could make some space. He saw the bruises on Jason's face.

'Your dad said you were down on your luck,' Mac said. 'But I didn't think I'd find you this bad.'

Jason lit a cigarette. 'I'm doing all right,' he replied. 'Dad should sort out his own life if he thinks he's so perfect.'

Mac went to the kitchen. He opened the fridge. 'This is disgusting!' he said. 'There's mould growing everywhere in here!' He slammed the fridge door shut.

Jason managed a smile. 'Who do you think you are?' he said. 'Gordon Ramsay?'

Mac grinned back. 'I'll be swearing like him if you don't get yourself sorted.'

Jason still felt dizzy. He sat on the edge of the sofa and stared at the stained carpet. His head pounded.

Mac picked up a handful of empty beer cans. They clattered as he threw them in the bin. 'What are you doing for money?' he said.

'Universal credit,' replied Jason.

'How about that lovely girl you were with?' asked Mac. 'She was a keeper.'

'Monica,' said Jason. 'That didn't work out.'

Mac shook his head. 'I'm not surprised,' he said. 'Look at the state of you. When was the last time you washed? Get yourself a shower, and I'll sort out some breakfast.'

What do you think?

- Why do Jason's cheeks glow when he thinks about the night before?
- What has changed in Jason's behaviour since his girlfriend threw him out? Why might this be?
- What does Mac think about the way Jason is living?
- How do you think Jason feels about himself and his life?
- If you were in Jason's situation, what could you do to feel better?

2
Happy as I am

Mac went out to the corner shop while Jason had a shower.

By the time Jason was dressed and ready, Mac had returned and started cooking. The flat was filled with the smell of grilled bacon and fresh toast.

Jason had to admit it felt good to be clean and shaved. And Mac had even sorted out the fridge. Bonus!

‘A bacon sandwich and a cuppa,’ Mac said. ‘You can’t beat it.’

They both tucked into their sandwiches.

‘Here’s the thing,’ Mac said. ‘Your dad has asked me to sort you out with a job.’

Jason stared at his bacon sandwich and said, ‘I’m not asking *him* for any help.’

Mac pulled some papers out of his pocket. ‘Well, I’m giving you help, if you’re asking for it or not,’ he said. ‘So listen up.’

He tapped the papers. ‘This is an application to work on the oil rigs as part of the maintenance team,’ he said. ‘It’s general labouring, like painting and fixing things. You’ve done your share of that in the past, and the money on the rigs is good.’

‘I won’t get the job,’ Jason said. ‘Why would they want me?’

'Because I'll put a good word in for you, you numpty!' Mac said. 'The bloke in charge of this is a mate.'

Jason picked up the papers.

'It's not an easy ride,' Mac said. 'You will have to pass a medical and a drugs test. And there will be a police check.'

Jason threw the papers back on the table. He felt his grip tighten on his mug of tea.

'What?' Mac asked. 'You haven't been in trouble with the police, have you?'

'I've had a couple of cautions,' Jason admitted.

'For what?' asked Mac.

'Scrapping,' said Jason. 'Just stupid brawls.'

'Well, all that has to stop,' Mac told him. 'You will have to get your act together.'

'I don't know,' said Jason.

'And you have to pass the HUET test,' said Mac.

'The what?' asked Jason.

'It stands for Helicopter Underwater Escape Training,' Mac explained. 'They strap you in a cage. Then they plunge you upside down into a freezing cold pool.'

Jason shook his head. He laughed nervously. 'I can't do that,' he said.

'You can do it,' Mac said. 'You have to if you want things to change.'

Jason felt his heart race. Just the thought of the underwater test made him feel a bit sick.

'You do want things to get better, don't you?' asked Mac.

Jason took a deep breath. 'Don't worry about me,' he said. 'I'm happy as I am. I'm not cut out for the oil rigs.'

Mac went to get his coat. 'Sleep on it,' he said. 'Give me a call in the week.'

'The answer is no,' Jason said. 'Thanks for the breakfast, but tell my dad to keep his nose out of my business.'

What do you think?

- Why does Jason feel a bit better at the beginning of this chapter?
- Jason says, 'I won't get the job. Why would they want me?' Why do you think Jason feels this way? Do you think he is right? Why or why not?
- Jason says, 'I'm happy as I am.' Do you think this is true? Why or why not?

- Could you boost your self-esteem (your opinion of yourself) by challenging some negative thoughts about yourself? For example, instead of thinking, 'I'm useless at everything,' think of things you are good at, like, 'I'm good at working with my hands.'
- What would you say to encourage a friend who was having similar negative thoughts to your own? Can you be as kind to yourself as you would be to your friend?

3
A second chance?

The next morning, Jason ran into his ex-girlfriend Monica in the street. She was wearing her gym clothes and some very expensive trainers. She was looking really fit.

Jason felt his stomach wobble when he saw that her golden hair was up in a ponytail. It was just the way he liked it.

'Hey, stranger,' Monica greeted him. 'I see you've run into a door again.'

Jason put his hand to his bruised eye. 'Something like that,' he said. 'You off to the gym?'

'I'm running Zumba classes at the gym. I'm earning good money and keeping fit,' she replied.

'Great,' said Jason, lighting up a cigarette.

Monica moved away from the smoke. 'What's new with you?' she asked him.

'Just the usual,' he said. 'My dad is winding me up.'

'How do you mean?' she said.

'He's nagging at me to get a job,' Jason said. 'Trying to get my uncle Mac to set me up with something.'

They walked together down the high street.

'That's not nagging,' Monica said. 'He's trying to help you.'

'Maybe,' muttered Jason.

'What's Mac got for you, anyway?' Monica asked.

Jason shrugged. 'Something out on the rigs,' he said. 'It's just maintenance stuff.'

'But that's great!' Monica said excitedly. 'Most people would jump at a chance like that.'

'Well, maybe I'm not most people,' Jason replied.

'No,' said Monica. 'You're a special type of idiot!'

Monica fixed Jason with a steady look. She put her hand on his arm. 'Give it a go,' she told him. 'Set yourself a target for once. Put everything back together again.'

They were standing outside a pub. Jason asked her, 'Do you fancy coming in for a drink?'

Monica shook her head. 'It's much too early for a drink. I'll see you around,' she said, and walked off.

Jason went into the pub and got himself a pint of beer.

Somehow, it didn't taste right. He looked around the bar. He saw the same old faces. He listened to the stories being told.

There were stories of missed opportunities. There were tales of chances that never quite came off. These men all had a past. But did they have a future?

Jason thought about Monica. Her hand had felt good on his arm. Would she give him a second chance?

Jason left his drink unfinished. He walked out of the pub and headed to the docks.

The port was busy. There were supply vessels being loaded up with food and equipment to take to the oil rigs. A helicopter flew low overhead.

Jason wondered whether he could be a part of that exciting world. Was he up for the challenge?

He took out his mobile and stared at it for a long time. Then he selected a number.

'Mac?' he said. 'It's Jason. I'll give it a go.'

What do you think?

- What does Monica think of Jason?
- Why doesn't Jason's pint of beer taste right?
- What makes Jason change his mind about the job?
- Jason says that his dad is nagging him. When have you felt like you were being nagged? Looking back, was it 'nagging' or was the person trying to help?
- Monica tells Jason to set himself a target. Why might this be good advice? What target could you set yourself?

4
Training up

Jason had found it difficult to make the decision to apply for the job, but that was just the beginning.

The training course to work on the rigs would cost about £1,000. That was a shock.

He would also need a certificate known as a BOSIET. This stood for Basic Offshore Safety Induction and Emergency Training.

Jason reached for his phone. His first thought was to ask his uncle Mac to loan him the cash. Mac was loaded, after all. That was the easy route. Jason had got into the habit of taking the easy way.

But something stopped him. Maybe it was pride. Or maybe it was just the feeling he had to stop relying on other people.

He went to the job centre and told them what he was planning. They were positive. There was money to help pay for training.

He also took a temporary job at the local supermarket to raise the rest of the money. He worked the late shift unloading the delivery trucks.

There were other changes Jason had to make.

He cut right down on drinking.

He packed in the online gambling. If he was honest with himself, he almost always lost anyway.

He stopped smoking as well. That was a tough one, but it saved a fortune.

The results were fast. In just a week he felt fitter. He slept better. He borrowed some weights from a mate and started working out. He went jogging for the first time in years.

It took a while, but at last Jason had enough money to start the course.

The training was full on. He had to practise fire safety drills and emergency evacuation procedures. He learned about sea survival and first aid.

It was a steep learning curve. And Jason hadn't been on a learning curve for a very long time.

He enjoyed it though. The other people on the course were a good laugh. Jason began to feel something he had not felt for a long time. It was the feeling of being proud of himself.

Finally, he came to the part of the course everyone was most worried about.

It was the helicopter escape training in the pool.

What do you think?

- What stops Jason from 'taking the easy way'? Why was or why wasn't this a good decision?
- Can you think of a time when you have taken the easy way? Did you regret it later? Why or why not?
- How is Jason feeling now compared with at the start of Chapter 1? What has made the difference?
- If you could train to do a new job or learn a new skill, what would it be? Is there anything you could do to make this happen?
- When have you done something that made you feel proud? In the future, what would make you feel proud?

5
The rig

Jason was strapped into the test rig. It was like being trapped in a metal cage.

He heard the sound of a siren. Then he heard the command, ‘Brace! Brace!’

Jason took a big breath as the test rig was dropped into icy water.

His heart pounded hard. The water was shockingly cold, and it shot straight up his nose. The urge to scream was almost too much.

Then the test rig flipped upside down. It felt like being in an action movie, or on a fairground ride that had gone wrong.

Jason tried to remember what he had been taught.

'Fight the panic,' the instructor had said. 'Focus on yourself. Don't worry about what anyone else is doing.'

He must find the window. Push it out. Unlock the seat harness. Pull himself out of the cabin.

Jason found it difficult to find the handle on the window when he was upside down. What if it didn't open?

He snatched at the handle, and the window popped out. He jabbed at the belt release. He swung his arms out.

Then somehow Jason was bobbing up on top of the water. He was safe. The whole thing had lasted less than fifteen seconds.

'Good work,' the instructor told the team. 'You've all passed.'

Jason sent a photo of his certificate to Monica.

She sent a message back. It read, 'You'll be out on the rigs before you know it.'

Her words gave him a warm buzz.

*

Two weeks later, Jason was on a helicopter flying over the North Sea. He was heading for his first job on a rig.

The flight took more than an hour. The ocean looked grey and stormy, but Jason felt excited as he saw the oil rig rising out of the ocean. There were huge flames shooting out of the rig's flare stack.

As soon as the helicopter landed, Jason liked the buzz of the rig. It felt like a ship. You could feel it moving in the sea. Massive waves slapped into the rig's steel legs. The wind whistled around it.

Jason thought it might take a while to get used to the noise. There was the sound of clanging metal, the hiss of compressors, a siren with a high-pitched wail and the shouts of the men on the drilling deck. He knew that the drilling would go on all day and all night.

The smell of the sea was in the air, along with the sharp stink of gear oil.

Jason and the other new workers were given a tour. They were shown where they could do their laundry, the games room with a pool table and TV, and the gym with some top-rate machines.

They were taken through the safety drills and given the work clothes and boots they would need.

They were told about the different teams on the rig. There were those who did the drilling, there were divers like Mac, there were welders and members of the fire team and the cook team. Then there were the 'roustabouts', like Jason, who did the painting and general maintenance.

Everyone on the rig had earned their place. Everyone had their special job.

It would be totally different from any situation Jason had ever been in.

He knew he had a lot to learn.

What do you think?

- How does Jason feel about the helicopter escape training? How would you feel if you had to take this test?
- Is Monica good or bad for Jason's self-esteem (his opinion of himself)? Why?

- Who helps to improve your self-esteem? Who brings it down? How could you build up relationships with people who are positive and appreciate you?
- What could you do to build up other people's self-esteem?
- Jason feels hopeful and confident when he lands on the rig. What could you focus on to help give you a feeling of hope and confidence?

6
A changed man

There were hundreds of men on the rig in the middle of the North Sea. There were some women too, especially among the engineers. It was like a small town.

Jason felt like a little kid on the first day of school. He was excited, but he also felt that he didn't belong.

Mac belonged, though. He knew everyone. The divers were the most respected people on the rig. They swaggered about like masters of the universe. But everyone had a kind word to say about Mac.

Jason met his foreman, who was called Rick. Rick was a friendly bloke from Bristol. He had a thick, rough beard and a West Country accent.

'Any mate of Mac's is a mate of mine,' Rick told Jason. 'Put your hours in and you'll do fine.'

Space was tight on the rig. Everyone shared a bedroom. They were called cabins, like on a ship.

Jason was sharing with Anish. Anish loved music and spent most of his time with his headphones on. He didn't say a lot and kept his side of the cabin clean.

Jason thought he would be easy to get on with.

So far, so good, he thought to himself.

Then, in the canteen, Jason locked eyes with a character from his past.

Gaz.

So far, so . . . bad.

Jason swore under his breath. Gaz was working on the cook team.

As soon as he saw Gaz, Jason's mind flashed back. He had bad history with Gaz.

Jason had grown up in Aberdeen with his younger brother, Sandy. Sandy was a lovely lad, but a bit soft. He didn't know how to say no. He had fallen in with Gaz and his gang. Somehow, Gaz never got nicked. Somehow, Sandy always did.

Sandy got three years in a young offender institute and a crushed leg when Gaz rolled a stolen car into a muddy ditch one night. Sandy had needed five operations on his leg, and it still wasn't right.

Gaz slapped some chicken stew on to Jason's plate. Gravy splashed on to Jason's trousers.

‘I’m surprised to see you out here,’ Gaz said. ‘Normally they’re a bit fussy about who they take.’

‘You can talk,’ Jason told him.

‘I’m a new man,’ Gaz said with a smile. ‘I’m the leopard that changed its spots, mate. What have they got you doing out here anyway?’

‘I’m on the maintenance crew,’ replied Jason.

‘Oh yeah?’ said Gaz. ‘Well as long as you know how to unblock a toilet, you’ll do fine.’

Jason moved on.

The stew was good, but it still stuck in his throat.

What do you think?

- Jason thinks Anish will be easy to share a cabin with. What would, or wouldn’t, make a good cabin mate?

- Would you like to work on an oil rig? Why or why not?
- Jason's brother Sandy found it difficult to say no to Gaz. Who do you find it difficult to say no to? What would happen if you did say no?
- What does Gaz mean when he says, 'I'm the leopard that changed its spots'? Do you think people can change who they are? Why or why not?

7
New friends, old enemies

After lunch, Jason started work. He and two other lads were painting the cabin doors in the accommodation block.

It was quite boring work, but Jason found himself enjoying it.

'Nice effort,' Rick, the foreman, told him.

It felt good to be praised.

Jason met Mac for a coffee in the canteen and gave him an update.

Mac was about to start some deep-dive projects. Jason wouldn't see him for a week, because his uncle would have to spend time in the decompression chamber so his body could adjust to normal air pressure.

Jason called Monica that night from his mobile. The Wi-Fi on the rig was really good.

'Sounds like you've made a good start,' Monica said.

They chatted for a while about this and that.

Then Jason heard a man's voice in the background. Jason felt his jaw tighten. 'Who's that with you?' he asked.

'Oh. That's Phil,' Monica said. 'He's moved into my place. I've been seeing him for a few months. He runs the gym where I work. I was meaning to tell you.'

Jason ended the call.

He felt a very long way from home.

*

A week went past. Jason focused on the painting. He tried not to think about Monica or her new bloke.

Luckily, the men on the paint team were a good bunch. There was a lot of banter and joking about. Jason found himself feeling better about stuff. Making new mates chased away the demons.

Then, not long after Mac had come off his dive job, Rick pulled Jason aside.

'Have you heard the news?' Rick asked him.

'What?' said Jason.

‘There’s been a theft,’ Rick said. ‘A diver’s watch worth seven grand has gone missing from one of the cabins. The watch belongs to Mac.’

Jason felt his fists curl up. Who could do that to Mac?

Rick gave Jason a strange look and said, ‘Problem is, you were the last one in those cabins, weren’t you?’

‘What?’ Jason said, stunned.

‘This could get messy,’ Rick said, and walked away.

From that day, everyone on the rig was talking about one thing only, and it was the theft of Mac’s watch. It was years since anything had been stolen on the rig.

Gaz could not stop talking about it. He yelled across the TV room to Jason that evening, ‘Hey, weren’t you working in that corridor where the watch got nicked? Just saying, like.’

The room went silent. It was packed with people who were off duty. Jason's face flushed red. He couldn't stop it.

'Yeah, I was,' Jason told him. 'I never saw anything dodgy.'

'Never *saw* anything,' said Gaz. 'But you had the master key to those cabins, didn't you, so that you could paint inside?'

'Yeah, I did,' Jason said. 'That doesn't mean I nicked anything, especially not from my uncle. Besides, most people don't bother locking their cabins anyway.'

By now, lots of people were staring at Jason.

Jason went to the gym. He pushed himself hard on the machines. He knew that Gaz was playing with his mind. But others had been listening.

The damage had been done.

What do you think?

- Jason enjoys working as part of a team. What is good or bad about working in a team?
- Why does Jason suddenly feel a long way from home?
- Why might it be important to keep in touch with family and friends if you are away from home? What are some good ways of doing it?
- Why might it have been years since anything on the rig was stolen? What does this say about the community on the rig?
- What do you think Jason might say or do the next time he sees Gaz? What advice would you give him?

8
On the edge

Jason could tell what the men were thinking. He could see it from the sideways looks he got. He could feel it from the whispered conversations that stopped as he walked by.

Jason's roommate Anish started locking his personal cupboard in their room.

Then Jason met up with Mac. His uncle was looking a bit grey in the face. His hand was shaking as he held his cup of coffee.

'This is bad news,' Mac told him.

'You don't think I did it, right?' Jason asked him.

Mac stared into his coffee cup. He couldn't look Jason in the eye. 'I don't know what happened to my watch, but I've stuck my neck out to help you get this job,' Mac said. 'Now there's bad blood and rumours flying around. It makes me look a bit of an idiot, don't you think?'

Jason didn't sleep that night. He was too wound up.

*

In the morning, Jason didn't want to shower. He didn't want to eat breakfast. He was so worried and stressed that he felt sick.

He couldn't even work. The men had said they didn't want him painting in their cabins.

After staring at nothing for a few hours, Jason called Monica. She answered straight away. It felt good to think he had at least one proper friend. They talked for ages.

‘I think you’re on the edge,’ she told him. ‘You need to find a way to chill. I can talk you through some breathing exercises.’

‘What good is that going to do?’ he asked.

‘You might be surprised,’ Monica said. ‘Come on, give it a go.’

Anish was working his shift, so Jason could do the deep breathing without feeling weird.

He lay on his back with his feet flat on the floor and his arms by his side. He followed Monica’s instructions as she talked him through the breathing exercises.

Five minutes passed. Then ten. It did help him feel better.

‘Another thing is to keep active,’ Monica continued. ‘Don’t stop going to the gym. In fact, you should go more!’

‘I’m just feeling angry the whole time,’ Jason told her. ‘I’ve been accused of a crime I didn’t do and it makes me feel like taking a swing at someone.’

‘Do not do that,’ Monica told him firmly. ‘That’ll just make things worse. Maybe they’ll get the police involved.’

Just before lunch, a security team came to Jason’s room.

‘I’m sorry we have to do this,’ Helen from the security team told him. ‘But you definitely had access to Mac’s cabin when the watch went missing.’

The security team didn’t say much. They looked in the cupboards and drawers. They searched the pockets of all Jason’s clothes. They even looked beneath the sink.

They did not find the watch.

Then they asked Jason to get up off the bed so that they could check under his mattress.

They found some adverts.

The adverts had been ripped out of newspapers. Each one was for a jeweller or pawn shop in Aberdeen that specialized in buying top-of-the-range watches. Watches exactly like the one that had been stolen from Mac.

'Can you explain these?' Helen asked. 'You must admit this doesn't look good.'

Jason felt his jaw clamp up. He couldn't get a word out. That's how gutted he was.

He had been set up. His job on the rig was over almost before it had begun.

'We're going to have to let you go,' Helen told him. 'We will fly you back to the mainland later today.'

Except they couldn't fly him back. That afternoon a violent storm rolled in.

The waves crashed higher, and the wind began to howl like a hungry wolf. The rig creaked. It trembled with the impact of the giant waves. It groaned as if in pain.

The drilling team got the worst of it. They staggered in from their shift, dripping with sea water and shivering with cold.

An announcement was made that no helicopters or supply vessels would be coming in until the storm stopped.

'How long will that be?' Jason asked Anish.

'I don't know,' Anish said. 'These storms can last ten days.'

Monica talked to Jason on the phone every day. She helped him to focus on the present moment, reminding him to note his thoughts and feelings, the way his body felt and the world around him. She said it was called mindfulness.

It sounded like fuzzy stuff to Jason until he tried it. He definitely felt his mood get better.

Somehow, he just had to try and keep his act together.

What do you think?

- How does Jason feel after his conversation with Mac? What makes him feel this way?
- What are some good things to do if you are having trouble sleeping?
- Why does Jason call Monica? How could talking about a problem to someone you trust be helpful?
- Has Monica given Jason good advice or bad advice? How can we tell if someone is giving us good advice or bad advice?
- Relaxation and mindfulness can help reduce stress. Have a go at the breathing exercise on page 63 and the mindfulness activities on page 66. How could you work one or more of these into your daily routine?

9
Public enemy

Jason was under strict orders. He wasn't allowed to leave his room for anything except to eat or go to the gym.

'It's for your own safety,' Helen told him. 'There's a lot of bad feeling about this theft.'

The storm still raged. No helicopters came in. The tension was eating away at Jason.

Monica told him to think positively. 'They'll find whoever really stole the watch,' she said. 'Someone will find out the truth and you'll get your job back. Just be patient and be positive.'

She sounded so certain, but Jason felt like he was about to explode.

Then a visitor came to Jason's cabin. It was the last person he expected. Gaz.

Gaz had just finished his shift. He looked relaxed and had a mug of tea in his hand.

'You're in trouble then,' Gaz said.

Jason looked away. He found a spot on the wall to stare at. 'It's got nothing to do with you,' Jason said quietly.

'Some idiots can't keep their sticky fingers off other people's stuff,' said Gaz. 'You'll get a good price for that watch back in Aberdeen.'

'Get out,' Jason said.

Gaz didn't go. Instead, he came into the room and sat on Anish's bed.

He frowned at Jason. 'All the men are talking about you,' Gaz said. 'They don't like stuff getting nicked on the rig. It creates a nasty atmosphere.'

Gaz pointed at Jason. 'It's all about trust out here,' he continued. 'And a bad apple like you upsets everything.'

'I've been stitched up,' Jason blurted out, 'and you know it better than most.'

Gaz's eyes narrowed to two slits. Then he stood up quickly, puffing out his chest. 'Are you accusing me?' he asked. 'We can have it out here and now if you like.'

Jason felt his blood rise. His fists curled into tight balls of anger.

Then he slowly let out his breath. He remembered what Monica had told him.

‘Don’t let them wind you up,’ she had said. ‘Don’t get pushed into a fight. If you do, you’ll never get your job back.’

Jason told Gaz, ‘Just leave. And don’t come back.’

‘Yeah well, there’s no hurry anyway,’ said Gaz. ‘The lads and I will catch up with you later, one Friday or Saturday night, back in town. We know where you drink.’

Gaz dropped his mug. It shattered, and hot tea splattered over the floor. ‘Whoops,’ he said. ‘Clumsy me.’

Then he was gone.

Jason cleaned up the mess.

The situation was hard. He couldn’t see how it was going to get better.

*

A few more days went by. The storm passed, and Jason was flown back to the mainland.

His mind was all over the place. He didn't know what he would do next. Mac wouldn't tell the police about the watch, but there was no way Jason would get another job on an oil rig.

The shift had changed on the rig. Most of the men Jason had met were heading back to Aberdeen for three weeks.

On Friday night, Jason was drinking on his own down near the docks.

Gaz walked into the pub with his mates. They had come looking for Jason.

As soon as Gaz and Jason locked eyes, there was no doubt things were going to kick off.

'You know why I'm here,' Gaz told him.

Jason downed the dregs of his beer. Gaz's mates were taunting him.

'Outside then,' Jason said, following them out.

The pub door slammed shut, and Jason lunged forward. Shouts rang out from the watching men. Gaz swung a fist. Knuckles crunched on the side of Jason's head.

Jason and Gaz fell off the pavement in a bundle, each punching the other.

A taxi swerved to avoid them. The driver blasted the horn.

Suddenly, a firm voice said, 'Pack it in!'

Jason felt a strong hand. It grabbed him from behind and pulled him up.

Jason spun around. It was Mac.

'Break it up,' Mac said. 'I've got news for you lads.'

Jason and Gaz stood there, puffing and panting. The other men went back into the pub.

Mac showed them his wrist. Something glittered in the streetlight.

'What the . . . ?' Gaz said.

Jason blinked.

It was the watch.

'Come with me,' Mac said. 'I'll tell you both what's happened.'

What do you think?

- What does Jason mean when he says to Gaz, 'I've been stitched up, and you know it better than most'?
- What helps Jason to keep control of his feelings when Gaz visits him in his cabin?
- Why does Jason fight with Gaz at the pub? What else could he have done?

- Monica encourages Jason to think positively. Can you think of some positive statements to apply to your life? For example, 'I can learn from this' or 'I am in control of how I react to others'.

- Looking back over today, can you think of three things that have gone well or three things you are grateful for? They can be simple things like, 'I enjoyed my cup of tea'. Challenge yourself to think of three things every day for a week, and see if it helps you feel more positive.

10
High pressure

They went to a cafe across the road. Mac got everyone a coffee. Then he took a deep breath and looked at Jason.

'I owe you a massive apology,' he said. 'Here's what happened. The thing is, I made a mistake after my last dive. I messed up on my pressure calculations. I didn't spend enough time in the chamber. I got narked.'

'What does narked mean?' Jason asked.

'Nitrogen narcosis,' Mac explained. 'It messes with the mind. It makes weird stuff happen. For some strange reason, I hid my watch behind my bunk in the pressure chamber. Then, when I left, I forgot to take it.'

The table was quiet.

'So, it was never stolen,' Mac said. 'I just made a mistake. It's as simple as that.'

Jason wanted to yell *'You see?'* at Gaz, but he kept silent.

Mac looked at Jason. 'I need to say sorry to you,' he said. 'It took a while for the watch to be found. My actions got you into a whole load of trouble.'

Jason nodded. He was relieved that the mystery had been solved.

He could be very angry with Mac right now for all the trouble his mistake had caused.

Or he could take a more positive attitude.

Jason took a deep breath. 'No problem,' he said to Mac. 'It's good to know what happened. It wasn't your fault.'

The three men were silent for a few moments.

Then Jason turned to Gaz. 'What about those adverts?' he said. 'The ones they found under my mattress?'

Gaz just stared at the table for a while. Then he spoke slowly. 'It wasn't just me,' he said. 'Anyway, we only did it for a laugh.'

Jason felt his coffee go down the wrong way. 'A laugh?' he said bitterly. 'You think it's funny to try and get me sacked?'

Gaz held up his hands. 'Chill,' he said. 'I agree it was out of order. I can see that now. I was just angry because I really thought you had nicked the watch.'

'You two need to stop this argument,' Mac told them. 'What's done is done, and you both need to move on.'

Jason stared hard at Gaz.

'I want you two to shake on it,' Mac said. 'Forgive and forget.'

Gaz held out his hand. After a moment, Jason shook it.

'I'll see you around,' Gaz said. Then he disappeared into the night.

Mac and Jason walked around the docks. It was as busy as ever, with the bright lights of the supply vessels beaming through the darkness.

'I've had a word with the rig team,' Mac said. 'They know you didn't do anything wrong. They said they will take you back.'

'That's really good news,' Jason told him.

Then Mac said, ‘But I’m not sure I’ll be diving for much longer. This mistake I made has got me thinking.’

‘How do you mean?’ Jason asked.

‘I’ve had a good run,’ Mac continued. ‘I’ve worked on rigs all over Asia and the Gulf of Mexico, as well as here. Now I think it may be time to quit.’

‘You mean you want to retire?’ asked Jason.

‘Exactly,’ said Mac. ‘I’ve built myself a nice pension. It feels like now is the time to enjoy it. Diving is a young man’s game.’

A couple of Mac’s team spotted him. They came over to chat.

‘Anyway, see you around,’ Mac said to Jason. ‘And keep out of trouble!’

Mac walked away with his mates.

‘Oh, by the way,’ he called back to Jason. ‘I ran into that ex-girlfriend of yours earlier.’

Jason felt his cheeks glow red. ‘Monica?’ he asked.

‘Yeah,’ Mac said. ‘She told me that she’s single again. Apparently, it didn’t work out with some guy from the gym.’

Jason smiled. ‘Ah, right,’ he said. ‘Thanks for telling me.’

Jason watched Mac walking away. He thought of all the amazing things his uncle had done in the Navy and when working on the rigs.

He thought about how Mac loved his wife and children, and about how loyal he was to them.

Mac always looked forward. He never looked back. He was a legend.

Jason wondered if people would be able to say the same about him when the time came for him to retire.

A helicopter clattered overhead as it made its way out into the darkness of the North Sea.

Jason got out his mobile.

He called Monica's number.

What do you think?

- Gaz says, 'We only did it for a laugh.' Why is or why isn't this a good reason? Who found it funny, and who didn't find it funny?
- Was Jason right to shake hands with Gaz? Why or why not? What would have happened if he hadn't shaken hands?

- What has Jason done, or not done, that makes it possible for him to go back to working on the rig now that they know he didn't steal the watch? How might this have worked out differently?
- How easy do you think it will be for Jason to go back to working on the rig? Why? What advice would you give him?
- Thinking back through the story, who has been kind and why? How does doing something kind make you feel? What could you do to be kind?

More ideas for discussion or writing

You could discuss these ideas in a group and then have a go at writing them down as a group or by yourself.

- The story ends with Jason about to call Monica. Can you think of three things Jason might say to her? What do you think Monica will say to him? You could write their conversation out like a movie script.

- Imagine that you are Jason and that you have just had your first day back at work on the oil rig. Write a short diary entry describing what it is like to be back. Is everyone pleased to see you? You might want to start: 'I just finished my first day back working on the rig. It felt . . .'
- Based on what you have read in the story, write a job description for a 'roustabout'. This is the name for someone who does the painting and general maintenance on an oil rig. What training or qualifications are needed? What does the job involve? What qualities does the person applying for the job need?
- Write your own short story called 'I only did it for a laugh' or 'The leopard that changed its spots'.

A breathing exercise

This breathing exercise can be done anywhere and takes just a few minutes. It can help relieve stress, anxiety and panic.

It will help you most if you do it often, maybe as part of your daily routine.

You can do it standing up, sitting in a chair that supports your back, or lying on a bed or mat on the floor.

Make yourself as comfortable as possible. If you can, loosen any clothes so you can breathe easily.

If you are lying down, place your arms a little bit away from your sides, with the palms up. Lie with your legs straight, or bend your knees so your feet are flat on the floor.

If you are sitting, place your arms on the chair arms or rest your hands on your thighs.

If you are sitting or standing, place both feet flat on the ground.

Whatever position you are in, place your feet roughly hip-width apart.

- Let your breath flow as deep down into your belly as is comfortable, without forcing it.
- Try breathing in through your nose and out through your mouth.
- Breathe in gently and regularly. Some people find it helpful to count steadily from one to five. You may not be able to reach five at first.

- Then, without pausing or holding your breath, let it flow out gently, counting from one to five again, if you find this helpful.
- Keep doing this for three to five minutes.

Mindfulness activities

Mindfulness is about paying attention to what is happening here and now, and not thinking about what happened before or what might happen next. It is about being aware of where you are and what you are doing without reacting to what is going on around you.

Mindfulness can help improve your mental well-being.

Here are some quick mindfulness exercises that you could try.

Fist clench

- Clench your fingers and thumbs to make a tight fist.
- Turn your hand so that your fingers and thumbs are facing up.
- Take a deep breath in and imagine breathing into your fist.
- Can you tell what's happened?

Become aware of your surroundings

This exercise helps you to focus on the here and now. Take your time with this and don't rush.

- Sit or stand quietly.
- Look around you and name three things you can hear.
- Name two things you can see. Try looking for things you don't usually notice.
- Name one thing that you can feel.

What can you hear?

This is another exercise that can help you to focus on the here and now, and it may help you to feel less wound up.

- Sit or stand still and name ten things that you can hear.
- What can you hear inside the room? What can you hear outside the room? What sound is coming from your body? Which sounds are louder than others?

Mindful tea or coffee drinking

When you drink a cup of tea or coffee, try doing it slowly and with care.

- What can you hear, smell, see, taste and feel?
- Think about this from when you reach out to pick up the mug to when you take the last mouthful. For example, you might note the shape of the mug, the smell of the drink and how hot it feels in your mouth.

Flat feet

- If you are feeling angry, try placing your feet flat on the floor. You can be sitting or standing.
- Breathe normally and do nothing.
- Think about what has made you angry and let yourself feel your anger.
- Now focus all your attention on the soles of your feet. Slowly move your toes. If you have socks and shoes on, how do they feel? If you have bare feet, how does the floor feel? How do your heels feel? And the arches of your feet?
- Keep breathing normally and focus on the soles of your feet until you feel calm.
- Now that you have controlled your anger, you can respond to what made you angry with a clear head.

If you need someone to talk to

The Samaritans (www.samaritans.org)

If you need someone to talk to, you could call the Samaritans.

Their free helpline number is: **116 123**.

The Samaritans offer a private and confidential listening service. You do not have to tell them your name. You can call them any time of the day or night for free. Calls from both landlines and mobile phones are free. If you are calling from a mobile phone, you do not need any credit or call allowance to make a call.

The Samaritans in prisons

If you are in prison, you can ask to speak to a 'Listener'. Listeners are prisoners who have been specially trained by the Samaritans. They can provide you with private and confidential emotional support if you are struggling to cope.

Also, all prisons must offer people in prison access to the Samaritans' free helpline: call **116 123**.

People to talk to if you are in prison

If you are in prison, you could also speak to a chaplain, even if you don't have a particular faith. Or you could speak to a member of the healthcare team or to staff on the wing.

Looking after your mental well-being in prison

Being in prison can be very difficult. The environment, the rules and the lack of control can all have an impact on your mental health. Ask the library if they have a copy of *How to look after your mental health in prison*, published by the Mental Health Foundation. This practical guide can be downloaded for free. Visit: www.mentalhealth.org.uk/publications/how-look-after-your-mental-health-prison

Books available in the Diamond series

Space Ark

by Rob Childs (ISBN: 978 1 908713 11 7)

Ben and his family are walking in the woods when they are thrown to the ground by a dazzling light. When Ben wakes up he finds they have been abducted by aliens. Will Ben be able to defeat the aliens and save his family before it is too late?

Snake

by Matt Dickinson (ISBN: 978 1 908713 12 4)

Liam loves visiting the local pet shop and is desperate to have his own pet snake. Then one day, Mr Nash, the owner of the shop, just disappears. What has happened to Mr Nash? And how far will Liam go to get what he wants?

Fans

by Niall Griffiths (ISBN: 978 1 908713 13 1)

Jerry is excited about taking his young son, Stevie, to watch the big match. But when trouble breaks out between the fans, Jerry and Stevie can't escape the shouting, fighting, and flying glass. And then Stevie gets lost in the crowd. What will Jerry do next? And what will happen to Stevie?

Breaking the Chain

by Darren Richards (ISBN: 978 1 908713 08 7)

Ken had a happy life. But then he found out a secret that changed everything. Now he is in prison for murder. Then Ken meets the new lad on the wing, Josh. Why does Ken tell Josh his secret? And could it be the key to their freedom?

Lost at Sea

by Joel Smith (ISBN: 978 1 908713 09 4)

Alec loves his job in the Royal Navy. His new mission is to save refugees from unsafe boats. But when a daring rescue attempt goes wrong, Alec is the one who needs saving. Who will come to help him?

Uprising: A true story

by Alex Wheatle (ISBN 978 1 908713 10 0)

Alex had a tough start in life. He grew up in care until he was fourteen, when he was sent to live in a hostel in Brixton. After being sent to prison for taking part in the Brixton riots Alex's future seemed hopeless. But then something happened to change his life . . .

You can order these books by visiting www.diffusionbooks.org.uk or by writing to Diffusion, SPCK, 36 Causton Street, London SW1P 4ST.

Books available in the Star series

Not Such a Bargain

by Toby Forward (ISBN: 978 1 908713 00 1)

Josh has everything worked out. He knows how to make easy money and he's got a sweet deal living with his mum. But when he meets the lovely Lisa, she starts asking questions that don't have good answers. And soon the police are asking too.

Barcelona Away

by Tom Palmer (ISBN: 978 1 908713 01 8)

Matt likes nothing better than a couple of pints while watching football with his mates. Actually being in the stadium when the action kicks off is even better. But a match can easily turn ugly, and soon Matt will have to decide between his love for the game and his love for his daughter.

Forty-six Quid and a Bag of Dirty Washing

by Andy Croft (ISBN: 978 1 908713 02 5)

Barry is looking forward to his first days out of prison. Free at last! He has nothing to lose but his £46 discharge grant, a bag of dirty washing, and all the promises he made to himself when he was inside . . .

Bare Freedom

by Andy Croft (ISBN: 978 1 908713 03 2)

Barry is trying to get used to life on the outside. All he wants is to make up with his sister and lead a normal life. But with no money, no job and the local drug dealer after him, will Barry be able to keep out of trouble?

One Shot

by Lena Semaan (ISBN: 978 1 908713 04 9)

Dan has got his life together. He's training as a plumber and he's the star of his local boxing club. But his life hasn't always been so good. When Dan is given the chance to get revenge on his abusive dad, will he take it? After all, he'll only get one shot. Can he make it count?

Nowhere to Run

by Michael Crowley (ISBN 978 1 908713 05 6)

What's a fair punishment for stealing a watch? It's 1788 and Jacob Jones has been sentenced to seven years' labour in Australia. The work is hot, hard and dangerous. Will Jacob find a way to escape? Or is there nowhere to run?

You can order these books by visiting www.diffusionbooks.org.uk or by writing to Diffusion, SPCK, 36 Causton Street, London SW1P 4ST.